You Can Tell a Fairy Tale

Little Red Riding Hood

For the two little monsters
in my life.

A TEMPLAR BOOK

First published in the UK in 2018 by Templar Publishing,
an imprint of King's Road Publishing,
part of the Bonnier Publishing Group,
The Plaza, 535 King's Road, London, SW10 0SZ
www.templarco.co.uk
www.bonnierpublishing.com
Illustration copyright © 2018 by Migy Blanco
Text and design copyright © 2018 by Kings Road Publishing

1 3 5 7 9 10 8 6 4 2

ISBN 978-1-78741-389-4

Designed by Genevieve Webster
Written and edited by Katie Haworth

Printed in Lithuania

YOU CAN TELL A FAIRY TALE

Little Red Riding Hood

Migy Blanco

templar
books

Have you met this girl before?

Red cape
for keeping warm
on long walks

Eyes
easily distracted
by butterflies
and flowers

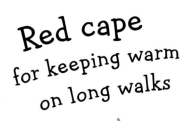

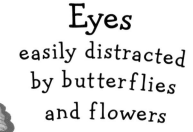

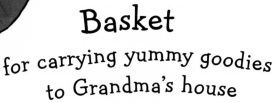

Very useful book
which she has forgotten
to read!

Pocket Guide
AVOIDING
WOLVES
VOLUME 1

Basket
for carrying yummy goodies
to Grandma's house

Sturdy boots
for walking through the
deep, dark forest

Oh, you have,
met her, have you?

What is her name then?

You guessed right!

This is
Little Red Riding Hood
and she needs someone
with a big imagination to
help tell her story.

Have you got a
big imagination?

Great!

Let's begin!

Once upon a time, there was a little girl who loved to wear her red cape, so everyone called her **Little Red Riding Hood.**

What else did she **really** like to wear?

She lived in a . . .

on the edge
of an enchanted
forest.

Today, Little Red's mum
has asked her to take a basket
of things to Grandma.

Can you find: 3 apples, 2 jars of jam and a pie?
Can you see anything else Grandma would like?

When Little Red Riding Hood gets outside, she looks at her map.

On her way through the trees, Little Red meets a **big bad wolf.**
Can you see anyone else in the forest?
"Where are you going, little girl?" the wolf asks.
"I'm visiting my grandma," says Little Red Riding Hood.

"How delicious . . . I mean, how nice!"
And the wolf smiles a toothy smile. "But why are you in such a hurry?
There are so many things for a clever young lady to do in the forest."

How does
Little Red Riding Hood
pass the time?

While Little Red is busy,
the wolf runs to
Grandma's house.
"I'm going to eat you up,
Granny!" he says.
"But first, I'm going to wait
for your pesky grandaughter
so I can eat
both of you!"

"Oh no you don't!"
says Grandma and she throws her . . .

at the wolf,
but it's no use. He bundles her into
a cupboard and **locks the door!**

Then he puts her cap over his big, wolfish ears, and opens up her wardrobe to choose something else to wear.

He puts on . . . .

Then he **hops** into bed and pulls the covers up.
A few moments later, Little Red Riding Hood
comes **skipping** in.

"Grandma!" she says. "What big . . .

you have!"

The wolf just smiles and says, "All the better to . . .

Smell

KISS

smile

DANCE

Hear

paint

K

KIC

See

wiggle

PARACHUTE

EAT

with."

(And remember, in the story Little Red asks three times —
so we have to go back to the top of the page and do it twice more!)

The wolf throws off the bed covers and snatches Little Red Riding Hood up. He locks her in the cupboard with Grandma and rubs his paws together.

Now it's time to make a wolfish feast!

In Grandma's kitchen the wolf starts cooking.
Can you find: 3 onions, 4 tomatoes and
salt and pepper? What else does he use?

FLOUR

Suddenly there is a knock at the door.

Someone has come to **save the day!** It's a . . .

They use it to send the wolf
far away to . . .

Little Red Riding Hood and Grandma are **safe!**

They say **thank you** to their new friend with a **gift** of . . .

When they get back to
Little Red Riding Hood's house,
they have a wonderful
fairyland ball to celebrate!

They invite all their friends.
How many of them do you recognise?

(Oh no! It looks like there is an uninvited guest!
Can you find him hiding somewhere?)

Thank you **so much** for telling this story!
Because of you, Little Red Riding Hood has made it home
safe and sound. Little Red has told the Queen of Fairyland
what you did and her majesty has awarded you
a precious golden . . .

Well done you!

More Picture Books from Templar:

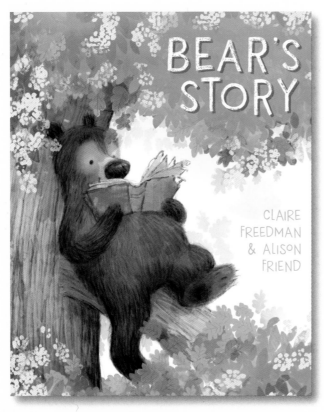

ISBN: 978-1-78370-644-0

ISBN: 978-1-78741-234-7

ISBN: 978-1-78741-073-2

ISBN: 978-1-78370-801-7